A Closer Look at Telescopes

by Judy Kentor Schmauss

HOUGHTON MIFFLIN HARCOURT

PHOTOGRAPHY CREDITS: 3 (b) ©Carlos Davila/Photographer's Choice/Getty Images; 6 (r) Comstock/Getty Images; 7 (t) ©Lloyd Sutton/Alamy Images; 7 (r) ©NASA; 9 (t) ©Ingram Publishing/Alamy; 9 (b) Michael Matisse/Getty Images; 11 (b) ©Photodisc/Getty Images

Printed in Mexico

ISBN: 978-0-544-07234-3

10 0908 20 19 18 17

4500669231 A B C D E F G

Contents

Vocabulary

moon
phases
telescope
magnify

Stretch Vocabulary

planet
rotate
lens
astronomer
refracting
reflecting
observatory

Introduction

It is a beautiful spring night. The sun has set. The moon is full. The stars are twinkling in the sky.

Do you ever wish you could see the moon or the planets close up? You can! And you do not need to ride in a rocket ship to see them better!

What would you like to see up close in the nighttime sky?

These moon phases take about 29 days.

The Nighttime Sky

People have been looking at the nighttime sky for thousands of years. They have watched the moon in all its phases. People have seen it turn from a new moon to a full moon. They have seen the stars change from season to season. People have wondered whether there is life on other planets.

From studying Earth, the sun, and the moon for thousands of years, we know many things. We know that Earth revolves, or goes around the sun. We know that the moon revolves around Earth.

People have figured out many things by looking at the sky. A telescope tells us so much more!

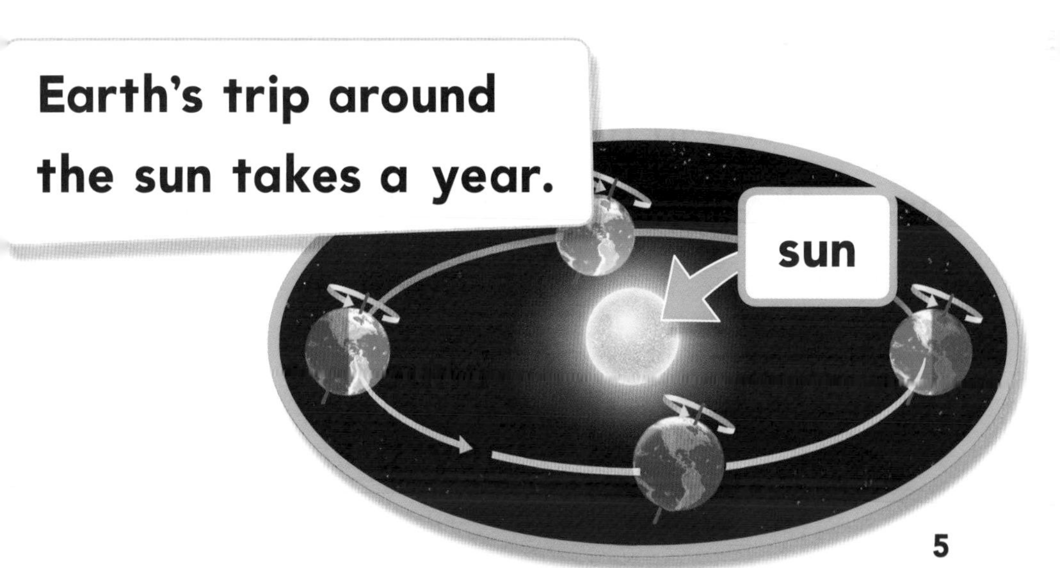

Earth's trip around the sun takes a year.

Galileo, the Scientist

If you have looked through eyeglasses, you know that eyeglasses change how you see. Glass lenses bend the light. Things look bigger.

An eyeglass maker invented the first telescope in the early 1600s. The eyeglass maker used a lens in his telescope to magnify things three times.

an early telescope

We can see many details with a telescope.

Galileo Galilei was an astronomer who lived long ago. An astronomer studies the objects in the sky. Galileo wanted to make his own telescope. He used a series of lenses. When Galileo finally finished, his telescope could magnify something to 30 times its size!

Types of Telescopes

A refracting telescope uses lenses. These glass lenses are curved. The light hits the curve and bends. The object looks bigger.

In a reflecting telescope, light hits a mirror and bounces to another mirror. The mirrors make the object look bigger.

Some telescopes use both lenses and mirrors.

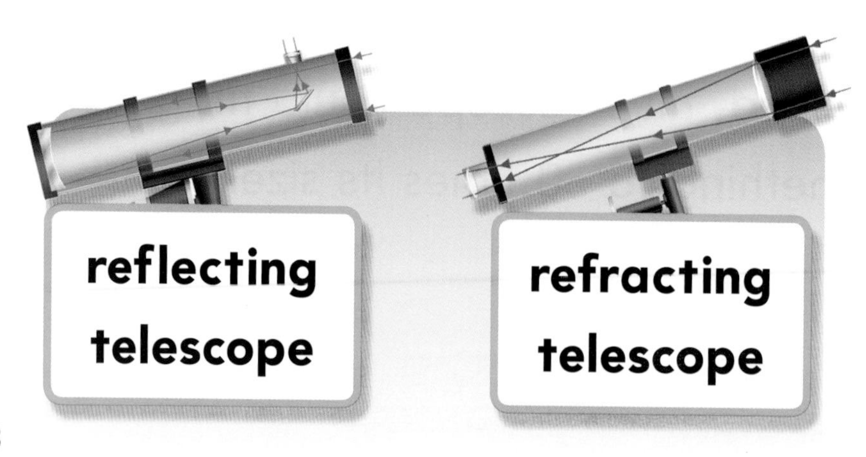

Using a Telescope at Home

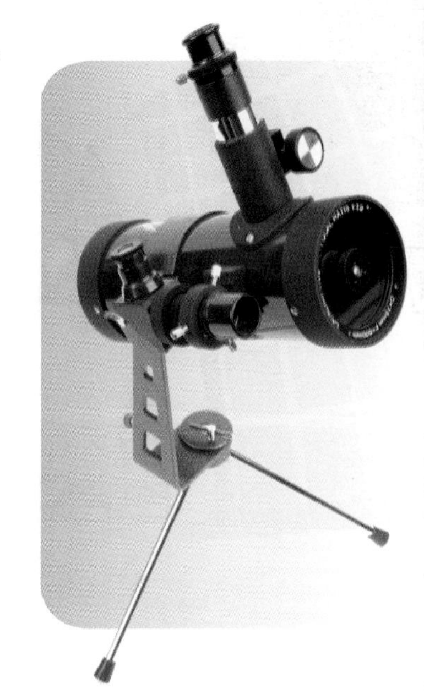

Telescopes come in many sizes. You may even have one of your own.

A refracting telescope is not as powerful as a reflecting telescope. It does not magnify objects as much.

Most home telescopes are refracting ones. Their smaller size makes it easier to move them around.

Telescopes come in many different sizes and styles.

This is an observatory.

Observatory Telescopes

An observatory is a place where astronomers study the sky. Observatory telescopes can be enormous! They can magnify something much, much more than home telescopes can.

The Hubble Space Telescope

In 1990, the United States sent the Hubble Space Telescope into space. It is an observatory above Earth! Thev telescope has cameras attached. The pictures that the Hubble sends back give us information and images we cannot get from observatories on Earth.

A telescope in space lets us see objects better than from Earth.

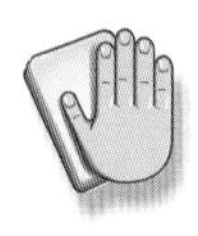

Magnify It!

Fill a glass with water. Put a pencil behind the glass and look at it through the water. Note what happens. Now put the pencil in the glass of water. Note what happens again. Talk with a partner about why you think the pencil looked different.

Write a Report

Use the Internet to look up magnification and how it works. Then write a report about what you learned.